For my good friends John and Helen
(and William, Bridget and Leo)
M.D.

For Emma O'Neill
Thanks to Mark, Lewis and Carlie and a debt
of gratitude to Philip, David and Eileen Pryce
at Cefn Saeson Fawr Farm in Neath
A.R.

SIMON &
SCHUSTER

First printed in Great Britain in 2002 by Simon & Schuster UK Ltd
Africa House, 64-78 Kingsway, London WC2B 6AH

Copyright © 2002 by Viacom International Inc.
Text copyright © 2002 by Malachy Doyle
Illustrations copyright © 2002 by Angelo Rinaldi

A CIP catalogue record for this book is
available from the British Library

ISBN 0-68982786-5

1 3 5 7 9 10 8 6 4 2

Printed in Hong Kong

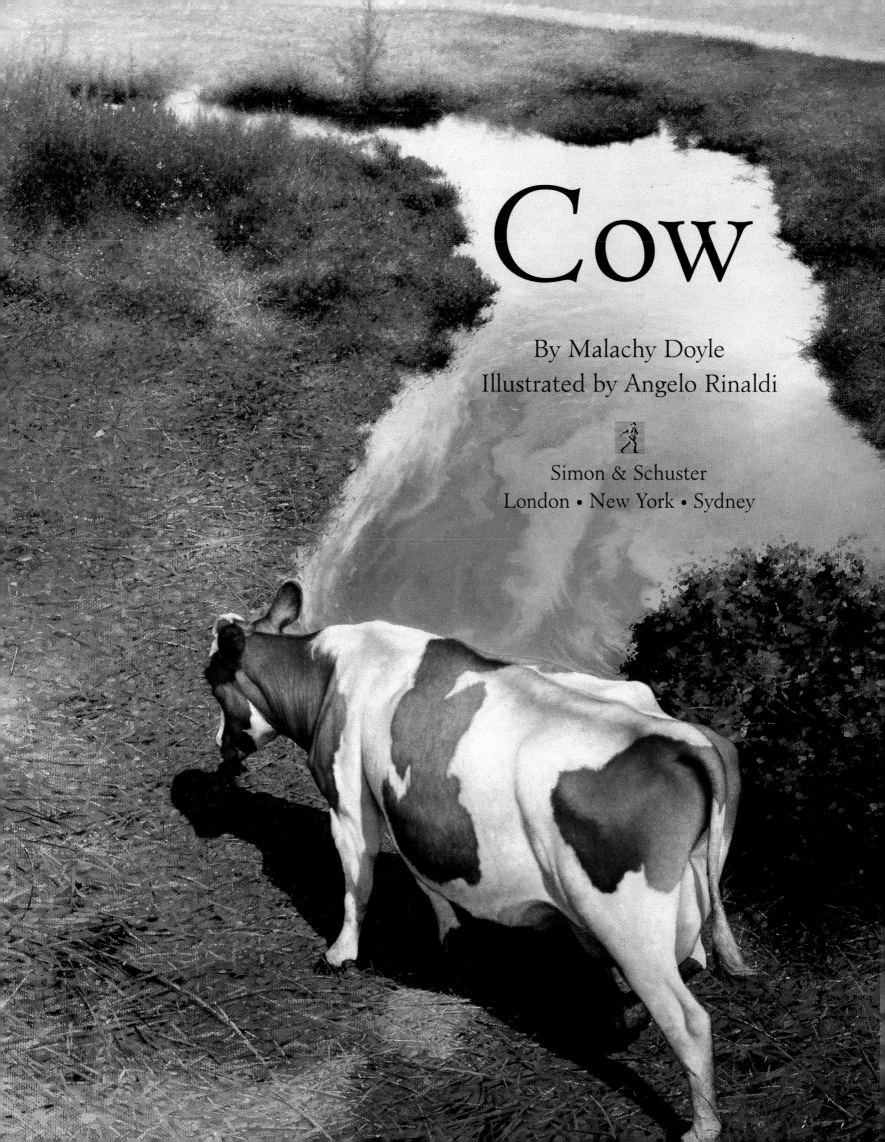

Cow

By Malachy Doyle
Illustrated by Angelo Rinaldi

Simon & Schuster
London • New York • Sydney

Cow.

Grazing in the field on a hot summer's day.

Early morning.
Dawn is breaking.
The first birds sing,
and the farmer strolls down the lane,

whistling.

Slowly you rise from the sodden grass,
your thick coat wet with morning dew.
Big and heavy,
you amble to the gate,
full udders swinging between your legs.

Past the sheep, resting in their field,
the pigs, dozing in their pens,

the gander, keeping guard,
and the farmhouse, where the children sleep.

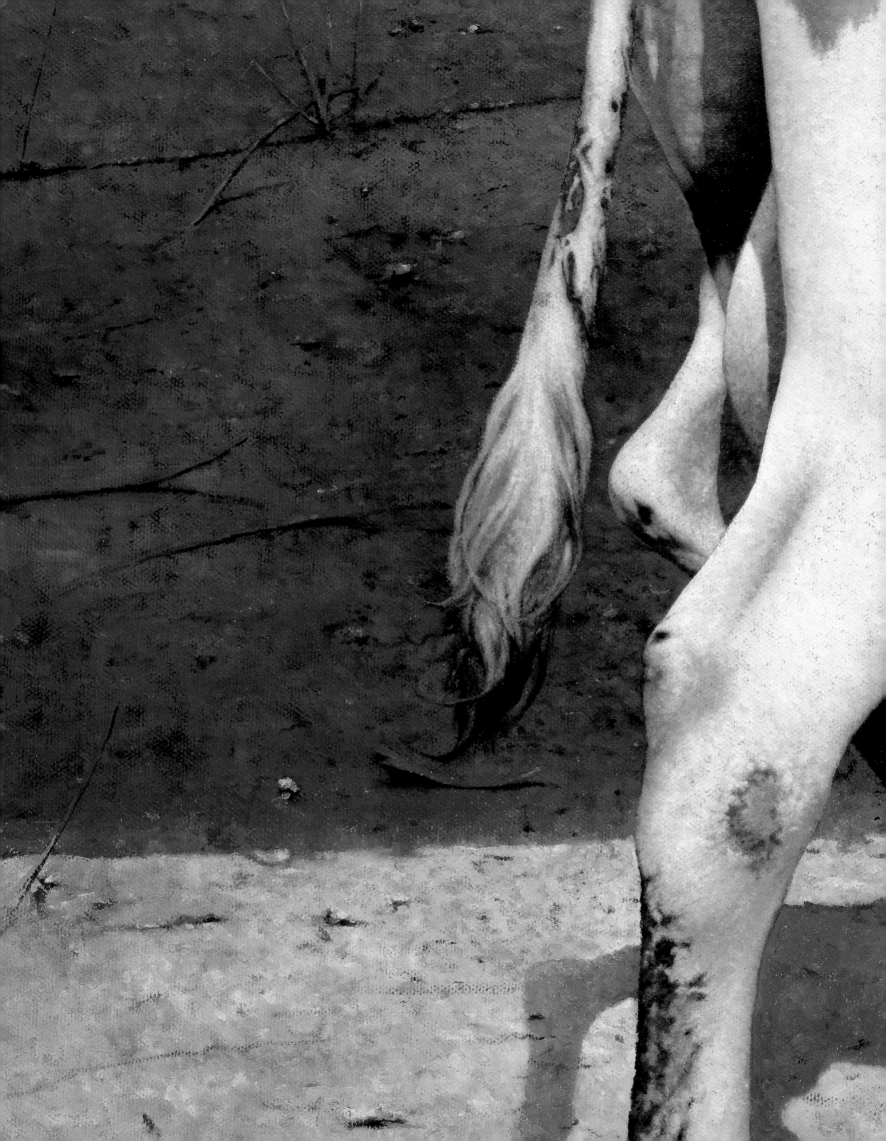

Your hooves click on the floor of the yard,
the gate opens and you enter the stall.

Food drops in front of you
and you bend to eat.
Gently the farmer cleans your udders,
and puts tubes on your teats.
Milk is sucked out, rich, warm,
creamy milk.

Then you wander back to the field.
Past the house, where the children are rising.
Past the coop, where the chickens are laying.

You tear the grass and chew the cud,
rolling your mouth from side to side.
Pushing the food with your thick, wet tongue,
over and over
for hours.

The school bus comes for the children,
the tanker arrives for the milk,
and slowly the morning passes.

The day warms up,
and your breath comes hot and heavy
from your broad wet nose.

You wander down to the river,
and take a long drink of the cool, clear water.

As the midday sun blazes,
you rest in the shade of the oak tree,
and close your deep, dark, eyes.
Your ears twitch to clear the flies from your face.
You swish them from your back with a long bushy tail.

The hot afternoon drags on, and the bus returns.
The children come to swing from the tree.
Out over the river,

and – splash! –

into the river.

Later you wait by the gate,
to be first in line,
your milk-full udders aching.

Lowing deeply as the farmer appears.

Pressing forward to the cool parlour at last.

You're back in the field.
The sun has gone.
The flies have flown,
and the long, hot day draws to an end.

You graze,

you chew,

and you rest.

It's hard work
being a cow.